BUF & MEAN JERRY BECOME FRIENDS

Created by Mack Zarling
Written by Dan Madson
Illustrations by Veronika Gonchar

Paperback ISBN: 978–1–952037–06–1
Ebook ISBN: 978–1–952037–07–8

Skrive publications

Skrive Publications
50 Surf Song Lane #413
Miramar Beach, FL 32550
www.skrivepublications.com.

This is Burgerhead.

He lives in a great big house
in a very small town.

Burgerhead has three dogs. No one knows how
Burgerhead can tell them apart, because all three
look exactly the same. They are identical dogs, and
they are very well behaved! They never bark at
strangers. They sit and stay.
And they come when they're called.

In Burgerhead's house is a great big refrigerator.
It's filled with his favorite food.
You probably think his favorite food will be burgers.
Don't you? Burgerhead's favorite food isn't burgers
at all! His favorite food is grapes. Yes,
grapes! That great big refrigerator,
bigger than any refrigerator you ever
saw, is filled with – GRAPES!

Burgerhead wears a basketball jersey and grey shorts. The number on his jersey is 34 because that's the number his favorite player wears.

Burgerhead has a long
blue bike with a banana
seat and high handlebars.
He rides his bike all
around the very small town where
he lives in a great big house with a
great big refrigerator.

This is Mean Jerry.

He lives in a very small house
in a great big city.

Mean Jerry has one dog. His dog is not well behaved at all. He barks at strangers. He digs holes in the back yard. And he never comes when he's called.

This is Mean Jerry's refrigerator.
Do you see how small it is? It's not like
Burgerhead's great big refrigerator. That's
because Mean Jerry doesn't have a favorite food.
And if you don't have a favorite food, you don't
need a great big refrigerator, do you?
In fact, Mean Jerry's refrigerator is empty.

Mean Jerry has an old red bike.
He got this old red bike from his neighbor
next door. Mean Jerry rides his old red bike all
around the great big city where he lives in a very
small house with an empty refrigerator.

One day, Mean Jerry moved from the great big city to the very small town. His new house was right next door to Burgerhead's house.

Burgerhead rode his long blue bike next door to greet his new neighbor.

"What's your name?" he asked Mean Jerry.

"Mean Jerry."

"Mean Jerry?" said Burgerhead. "Why are you called Mean Jerry?"

"It's just a nickname," said Mean Jerry. I'm not actually mean at all. My mom says that I just forget to be nice sometimes."

"What's your name?" asked Mean Jerry.

"Burgerhead," said Burgerhead "Burgerhead?" said Mean Jerry. "Why are you called Burgerhead?

"Because my head looks like a burger," said Burgerhead.

Why are you wearing such fancy clothes?" asked Burgerhead.

"My dad says that clothes make the man," said Mean Jerry.

"What does that mean?" said Burgerhead

"I'm not sure," said Mean Jerry, "but I think it means that if I wear fancy clothes, I'll grow up to be a great man."

"My dad says things like that too," said Burgerhead.

"Why are you wearing a basketball jersey?" asked Mean Jerry.

"I love basketball and I practice all the time," said Burgerhead. "My dad says that practice makes perfect."

"What does that mean?" asked Mean Jerry.

"I'm not sure," said Burgerhead, "but I think it means that if I practice enough I'll grow up to be a basketball star."

"Is that your dog?" asked Burgerhead. "What do you call him?"

"His name is Bert," said Mean Jerry.

"Why is he wearing a patch?" asked Burgerhead.

"He only has one eye," said Mean Jerry.

"Is that the only dog you have?" asked Burgerhead.

"Isn't one dog enough?" said Mean Jerry. "How many dogs should a guy have?"

Burgerhead tapped his finger on his basketball jersey and said, "I have three dogs."

"Three?" said Mean Jerry.

"Why would anyone have three dogs?

Burgerhead had never been asked that question before and wasn't sure what to say.

Mean Jerry said, "Having a dog is good. A dog never argues or talks back or says nasty things. Everybody should have a dog. ONE dog."

Burgerhead held up a finger up in the air as if he had a very important point to make. "If having one dog is good," he said, "having two dogs must be better. And having THREE dogs must be best of all!"

"What do you call your dogs?" said Mean Jerry.

"Four, Five and Six," said Burgerhead.

"Four, Five and Six aren't names," said Mean Jerry. "Those are numbers!"

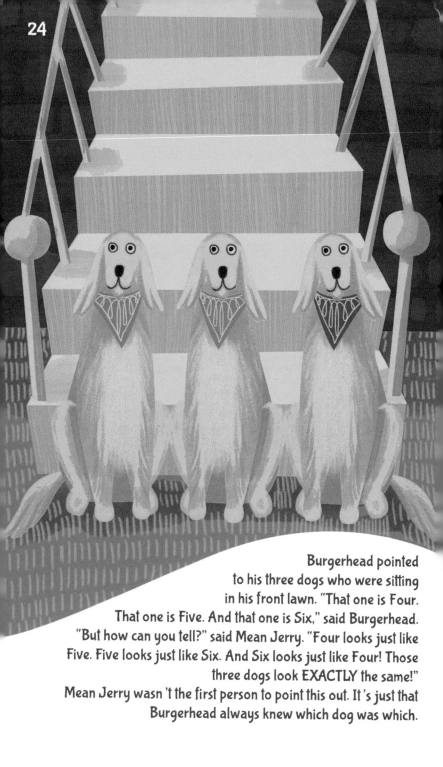

Burgerhead pointed
to his three dogs who were sitting
in his front lawn. "That one is Four.
That one is Five. And that one is Six," said Burgerhead.
"But how can you tell?" said Mean Jerry. "Four looks just like
Five. Five looks just like Six. And Six looks just like Four! Those
three dogs look EXACTLY the same!"
Mean Jerry wasn't the first person to point this out. It's just that
Burgerhead always knew which dog was which.

"Do you have a bike?" asked Burgerhead.

"Yes," said Mean Jerry. "I have an old red bike that a neighbor at my last house fixed up and gave to me."

"I have a long blue bike with a banana seat and high handlebars," said Burgerhead, pointing at his bike. "Let's go for a ride!"

Burgerhead and Mean Jerry jumped on their bikes
and went for a ride. They rode past Mr. Rodman's
house who lived next door. They rode past Mrs.
Hinckley's house who lived across the street. They
rode past the grade school. They rode past the
swimming pool. They rode past the Little League
diamonds. They rode past the park by the river with
the World War II airplane on display.

As they turned for home, a squirrel ran across the street in front of them. Burgerhead looked back at Mean Jerry and yelled, "Watch out! Squirrel!" Burgerhead swerved to avoid the squirrel, but Mean Jerry turned his bike right toward the squirrel. Luckily, the squirrel jumped out of the way and scampered up a tree.

Instead of hitting the squirrel, Mean Jerry hit a rock that was in the street. His old red bike went flying. When it landed, it cracked in half, right down the middle of the frame. Mean Jerry landed next to it with a thud.

Burgerhead stopped and went back to see what happened.

"Are you okay?" asked Burgerhead.

"My knees are scraped, but I'm okay," said Mean Jerry.

Burgerhead helped Mean Jerry pick up his
broken bike, and they walked back to his house.
Burgerhead pushed his long blue bike and carried
half of the broken bike. Mean Jerry walked slowly
carrying the other half of his bike.

"It's a good thing you didn't hit that squirrel,"
said Burgerhead. "Squirrels have feelings too,
you know."

Burgerhead and Mean Jerry set the broken pieces of the old red bike inside Mean Jerry's garage.

"I'll need a new bike," said Mean Jerry, "because now there's no neighbor to fix it."

"You could buy a new bike," said Burgerhead. "We'll both need bikes if we are going to share adventures together!"

"Where did you get your bike?" asked Mean Jerry.

"I bought it with my own money at the bike shop in town." said Burgerhead.

"Where did you get money," asked Mean Jerry.

"I helped out on my uncle's farm and saved enough money to buy a new bike!" said Burgerhead.

"Do you think I could help out on your uncle's farm?" asked Mean Jerry.

"Sure!" said Burgerhead. "I don't think he would mind at all!"

Burgerhead hopped on his long blue bike with a banana seat and high handlebars and rode back home. Mean Jerry went inside and told his mom he had made a new friend.

"I'm glad you made a new friend," she said. "Burgerhead's mom came over and brought us something to eat."

Mean Jerry was hungry, so he went to
the refrigerator and opened the door.
Can you guess what he saw?

Yes, inside the refrigerator was
a huge bowl of grapes!

Burgerhead and Mean Jerry
Become Friends
Making a new friend is a great thing!
Meet Burgerhead and Mean Jerry!

Burgerhead and Mean Jerry
Visit The Farm
A trip to the farm has Burgerhead and
Mean Jerry wrangling chickens!

About the Creator
of the Characters
Mack Zarling is the six-year-old
grandson of the author. He likes rockets,
sharks and baseball. Mack came up with
the premise of the characters and settings.
Like most kids, he loves a good story!

About the Author
Dan Madson is a former middle-school
teacher and coach. He's the author of five
books. This is his first book for children.
All the Burgerhead and Mean Jerry
stories are loosely based on exploits from
his childhood. He lives with his wife in
Florida, and his favorite food is popcorn

About the Illustrator
Veronika is an accomplished
artist/illustrator from Belarus.